NICKELODEON®

SpongeBob SquarePants®

VOTE for SPONGEBOB

by Erica Pass
illustrated by Harry Moore

SCHOLASTIC INC.

New York Toronto London Auckland Sydney
Mexico City New Delhi Hong Kong Buenos Aires

Based on the TV series *SpongeBob SquarePants*® created by Stephen Hillenburg as seen on Nickelodeon®

ISBN-13: 978-0-545-04147-8
ISBN-10: 0-545-04147-3

12 11 10 9 8 7 6 5 4 3 2 1   8 9 10 11 12 13/0

Printed in the U.S.A.

First Scholastic printing, September 2008

It was a day like any other at the Krusty Krab. SpongeBob was frying. Squidward was grumbling. And Mr. Krabs was counting his money.

"Barnacles!" he said. "We've come up short again! I need me a moneymaking plan, and I need one quick."

Mr. Krabs decided to look around the restaurant for ideas. First he went up to a well-dressed lady. "Enjoying your Kelp Patty, ma'am?" he asked.

"It's fine, but—," the lady started to say.

But Mr. Krabs wasn't listening. "Wonderful! Come again!" he said, as he scooted over to a woman with a little boy. The boy had a crown on his head.

"Say, sonny," said Mr. Krabs, "that's quite a crown you have there."

"I'm a king," the boy declared.

"He wears the crown everywhere," added the boy's mother. "People always ask about it."

"They do?" asked Mr. Krabs.

"Oh, sure," the woman answered. "People love royalty—you know, kings, queens, princesses, all that stuff."

"Is that so?" said Mr. Krabs. An idea was starting to brew in his mind.

Customers will flock to the Krusty Krab when they see what I have in store for them," said Mr. Krabs, as he walked away. "We're going to have ourselves a royal election!"

Mr. Krabs called SpongeBob and Squidward together. "Boys, it has come to my attention that we need some pizzazz around here," he announced.

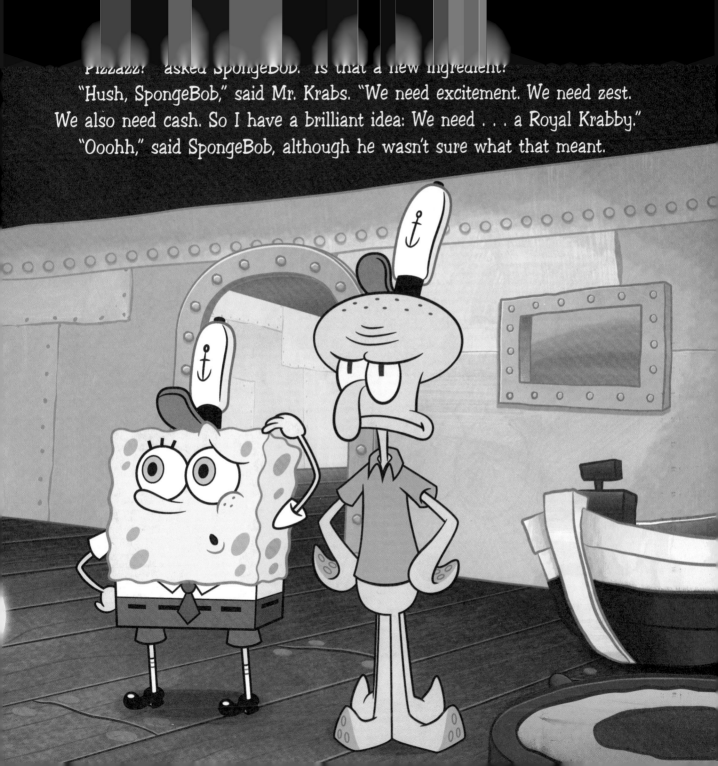

"Pizzazz?" asked SpongeBob. "Is that a new ingredient?"

"Hush, SpongeBob," said Mr. Krabs. "We need excitement. We need zest. We also need cash. So I have a brilliant idea: We need . . . a Royal Krabby."

"Ooohh," said SpongeBob, although he wasn't sure what that meant.

The Krusty Krab is going to have an election," Mr. Krabs explained. "And the two of you have been chosen to run for office. The one who gets the most votes will be our very first Royal Krabby!"

"Ooohh," SpongeBob repeated.

"This is your best idea yet, Mr. Krabs," said Squidward, not excited at all. "Look, I've already made your very first election poster!" said Mr. Krabs. "People can vote whenever they come into the Krusty Krab. So snap to it, boys. Get out there and tell everyone to vote for you!"

"Isn't this exciting, Squidward?" said SpongeBob. "One of us will get to be the very first Royal Krabby!"

"Thrilling," said Squidward.

"I just want you to know that even though things might get heated on the campaign trail, nothing will ever get in the way of our friendship," said SpongeBob. "May the best Krusty Krab employee win!"

SpongeBob couldn't wait to share the news with Patrick.

"Patrick!" said SpongeBob. "I'm running for Royal Krabby!"

"What's a Royal Krabby?" asked Patrick.

"Good thinking, Pat!" said SpongeBob. "We'll need to tell the public about the Royal Krabby. You're the perfect campaign manager. You're hired!"

"Okay, as my campaign manager, you're responsible for getting my name out there," said SpongeBob. "The public should know and love me. We'll need posters. And buttons—lots of buttons, with my face on them. And a parade. Everyone loves a parade!"

"It's true!" said Patrick. "I love a parade!"

SpongeBob and Patrick stayed up all night making buttons, posters, and flyers. They plastered VOTE SPONGEBOB FOR ROYAL KRABBY posters all over Bikini Bottom.

The next day SpongeBob and Patrick arrived at the Krusty Krab, where they covered the walls with posters. They ran past Squidward, covering him, too.

"SpongeBob!" yelled Squidward. "Get these off of me!"

"Sorry, Squidward," said SpongeBob. "I didn't mean to rub my campaign in your face. Patrick, please remove the poster from Squidward."

"Sure thing, boss," said Patrick.

"Ah, son," said Mr. Krabs when he saw SpongeBob. "I've been looking for you."

"Did you want to discuss official election business?" asked SpongeBob.

"No," said Mr. Krabs. "I want to discuss official work business. Mainly that you're supposed to be doing it."

"Oh, Mr. Krabs," said SpongeBob. "I'm too busy campaigning."

And before Mr. Krabs could reply, SpongeBob was already out the door.

SpongeBob and Patrick went door-to-door so they could get more people to vote for SpongeBob.

"What are you selling?" asked one man.

"Oh no, sir," said SpongeBob. "I'm running for Royal Krabby. And I would be grateful if you would go to the Krusty Krab to vote for me."

"Let me give you a hint, sponge," said the man. "You need to make some promises about what you're going to do if you want to be elected. That's how things work." He shut the door.

"Patrick," said SpongeBob, "I need to come up with some promises!"

SpongeBob spent the next week campaigning across town, making promises to everybody:

"As Royal Krabby, I will have all stores open twenty-four hours a day."

"As Royal Krabby, I will babysit your children."

"As Royal Krabby, I will install more stop signs."

He told people whatever he thought they wanted to hear.

"VOTE FOR SPONGEBOB"

Back at the Krusty Krab business was booming, but Mr. Krabs was not happy. Everyone was coming in to vote for Royal Krabby. Yet SpongeBob was still nowhere to be found. He was so busy trying to win the election that he had forgotten about the Krusty Krab itself!

Mr. Krabs needed SpongeBob back. He decided to call him in.

"You know, SpongeBob," said Mr. Krabs when SpongeBob arrived, "one of the finest qualities of a Royal Krabby is the love he has for his kingdom, the Krusty Krab. He loves to be in his kingdom as much as possible."

"Yes, Mr. Krabs," said SpongeBob. "But my world has become so much larger now—and my people need me."

"Well, we need you here, too," said Mr. Krabs. "And I have a surprise."

"A surprise?" asked SpongeBob.

"Yes," said Mr. Krabs. "The election is over! I'm going to tally the votes!"

"But Mr. Krabs," said SpongeBob. "I haven't finished campaigning! I still have to have a rally, and a debate with Squidward, and the parade—"

"Sorry," said Mr. Krabs. "It's decision time." He disappeared into his office to count the votes.

A few minutes later Mr. Krabs emerged. "And the winner is . . .

SpongeBob!" he said. "Congratulations! Here's your royal scepter. Now get to work."

"But Mr. Krabs," said SpongeBob, "don't I have special duties?"

"Of course," said Mr. Krabs. "You're responsible for making everyone who steps foot into the kingdom of the Krusty Krab feel welcome. You make sure that the Krabby Patties are edible and that the kingdom is always clean."

"What about all those promises I need to fulfill?" asked SpongeBob.

"You can fulfill them after work," said Mr. Krabs.

"Mr. Krabs, sir," said SpongeBob. "As your first Royal Krabby, I will do you and the people of Bikini Bottom proud. I will not disappoint."

"That's fine," said Mr. Krabs. "You can even have a dish named after you: the Royal Krabby Patty."

"With fried sea onions and extra pickles?" asked SpongeBob.

"Whatever you like," said Mr. Krabs, "as long as I can charge extra."

"Yippee!" said SpongeBob. "I'm going to get to work right now!"

SpongeBob returned to the kitchen. "Royal Krabby here, reporting for duty!"

"Do me a favor," said Mr. Krabs to Squidward. "The next time I say I have a brilliant idea, tell me to keep my mouth shut."

"With pleasure, sir," said Squidward.